A Note to Parents

Welcome to REAL KIDS READERS, a series of phonics-based books for children who are beginning to read. In the classroom, educators use phonics to teach children how to sound out unfamiliar words, providing a firm foundation for reading skills. At home, you can use REAL KIDS READERS to reinforce and build on that foundation, because the books follow the same basic phonic guidelines that children learn in school.

Of course the best way to help your child become a good reader is to make the experience fun—and REAL KIDS READERS do that, too. With their realistic story lines and lively characters, the books engage children's imaginations. With their clean design and sparkling photographs, they provide picture clues that help new readers decipher the text. The combination is sure to entertain young children and make them truly want to read.

REAL KIDS READERS have been developed at three distinct levels to make it easy for children to read at their own pace.

- LEVEL 1 is for children who are just beginning to read.
- LEVEL 2 is for children who can read with help.
- LEVEL 3 is for children who can read on their own.

A controlled vocabulary provides the framework at each level. Repetition, rhyme, and humor help increase word skills. Because children can understand the words and follow the stories, they quickly develop confidence. They go back to each book again and again, increasing their proficiency and sense of accomplishment, until they're ready to move on to the next level. The result is a rich and rewarding experience that will help them develop a lifelong love of reading.

To Bryan Tidd for creating this story, and to his
godfather, Richard Hartz (aka Uncle Rich),
for living it—L. V. T.

For James, with love
—D. H.

Special thanks to Lands' End, Dodgeville, WI,
for providing clothing and bedding.

Copyright © 1999 by Millbrook Press

Produced by DWAI / Seventeenth Street Productions, Inc.
Reading Specialist: Virginia Grant Clammer

Real Kids Readers and the Real Kids Readers logo are trademarks of Millbrook Press

Millbrook Press
A division of Lerner Publishing Group
241 First Avenue North
Minneapolis, MN 55401 U.S.A.

Website address: www.lernerbooks.com

Library of Congress Cataloging-in-Publication Data

Tidd, Louise.
   I'll do it later / by Louise Vitellaro Tidd ; photography by Dorothy Handelman.
       p.   cm. — (Real kids readers. Level 2)
   Summary: Rick has a week to complete a big homework assignment but keeps putting it
off in favor of other, more enjoyable activities.
   ISBN-13: 978–0–7613–2066–1 (lib. bdg. : alk. paper)
   ISBN-10: 0–7613–2066–0 (lib. bdg. : alk. paper)
   ISBN-13: 978–0–7613–2091–3 (pbk. : alk. paper)
   ISBN-10: 0–7613–2091–1 (pbk. : alk. paper)
   [1. Homework—Fiction.] I. Handelman, Dorothy, ill. II. Title. III. Series.
PZ7.T4345Il 1999
[E]—dc21   98–56274

Manufactured in the United States of America
6 7 8 9 10 11 – DP – 10 09 08 07 06 05

I'll Do It Later

By Louise Vitellaro Tidd
Photographs by Dorothy Handelman

Millbrook Press • Minneapolis

Rick came home from school
on Friday.
"Mr. Scott gave us extra homework,"
he told his mom.
"I have to draw a map of my street.
I have to bring it in next Friday."

4

5

"You have a basketball game
on Thursday," said Mom.
"Do you want to start your map now?"
"No way!" said Rick. "I want to play.
I have lots of time for my map.
I'll do it later."

On Saturday, Mom saw Rick
at his desk.
"Are you working on your map?"
she asked.
"No," said Rick.
"I am working on monsters.
I'll do my map later."

On Sunday, Rick went to
his friend Greg's house to play.
Greg was done with his map.
He showed it to Rick.

"You did a good job," said Rick.
"I will do a good job on my map too.
But I will do it later."

On Monday, Rick stayed after school
to shoot baskets with his team.
He got home just in time for dinner.
Then, after dinner, he read a book.
"I'll do my map later," he told himself.
"I still have lots of time."

On Tuesday after school,
Rick played with his toys.
"How about working on your map?"
said Mom.

"Sorry, Mom. I can't," said Rick.
"Robots are taking over the world,
and I have to stop them.
I'll do the map later."

On Wednesday, Rick came home
from school with lots of homework.
"I can't do my map now,"
he told Mom.
"I have too much other stuff to do.
I will have to do the map later."

The next day was Thursday.
Rick came straight home from school.
He got out markers and paper.
"I will do my map," he told himself.
"But first I need something to eat."
He made a snack.
It was very good.

A car horn beeped.
"Rick!" Mom called.
"Are you ready for the big game?
Your ride is here."
"Oh, no! Already?" said Rick.
He put on his coat.
He grabbed his gym bag
and ran for the door.
It was time to play basketball.
The map would have to wait.

Rick got home late.
His team had won,
and they had all gone out for pizza.
But Rick was not happy.
He had no time left to draw his map.
"I kept thinking I could do it later,"
he told Mom.
"But now there is no more 'later.'"

Rick went to bed.
He did not sleep very well.
He had not done his map.
What would Mr. Scott think?
The next morning Rick was still upset.
Slowly he got up.
Then Mom called to him,
"Rick! Take a look outside."

What a shock!
It had snowed in the night.
It had snowed a lot!
"School is closed," Mom told Rick.
Rick jumped up and down.
"Hooray!" he yelled.
"I can play in the snow!
But first I will draw my map!"

Rick did not stop to get dressed.
He ate as fast as he could.
Then he got out markers and paper.
He started to draw his map.
Just then the phone rang.
It was Greg.

"Hi, Rick," said Greg.
"Do you want to play in the snow?"
"I can't," said Rick.
"I'm working on my map."

"School is closed," said Greg.
"You can do the map later."
"No way!" said Rick.
"I'm going to do it now!
But I'll come out and play later—
I mean *soon*."
And that's just what he did.

Phonic Guidelines

Use the following guidelines to help your child read the words in *I'll Do It Later.*

Short Vowels

When two consonants surround a vowel, the sound of the vowel is usually short. This means you pronounce *a* as in apple, *e* as in egg, *i* as in igloo, *o* as in octopus, and *u* as in umbrella. Short-vowel words in this story include: *bag, bed, big, but, did, got, had, him, his, job, lot, map, mom, put, ran.*

Short-Vowel Words with Consonant Blends

When two or more different consonants are side by side, they usually blend to make a combined sound. In this story, short-vowel words with consonant blends include: *bring, desk, fast, grabbed, Greg, jumped, just, kept, left, next, rang, Scott, started, stop, went.*

Double Consonants

When two identical consonants appear side by side, one of them is silent. In this story, double consonants appear in the short-vowel words *dressed, still, stuff, well, will* and in the *all*-family words *all* and *called.*

R-Controlled Vowels

When a vowel is followed by the letter *r*, its sound is changed by the *r*. In this story, words with *r*-controlled vowels are: *are, car, for, horn, start.*

Long Vowel and Silent E

If a word has a vowel and ends with an *e*, usually the vowel is long and the *e* is silent. Long vowels are pronounced the same way as their alphabet names. In this story, words with a long vowel and silent *e* include: *ate, came, gave, home, late, made, phone, ride, take, time.*

Double Vowels

When two vowels are side by side, usually the first vowel is long and the second vowel is silent. Double-vowel words in this story include: *beeped, coat, eat, need, sleep, stayed, street, team, wait, way.*

Diphthongs

Sometime when two vowels (or a vowel and a consonant) are side by side, they combine to make a diphthong—a sound that is different from long or short vowel sounds. Diphthongs are: *au/aw, ew, oi/oy, ou/ow*. In this story, words with diphthongs include: *about, down, draw, house, how, now, out, saw, toys.*

Consonant Digraphs

Sometimes when two different consonants are side by side, they make a digraph that represent a single new sound. Consonant digraphs are: *ch, sh, th, wh*. In this story, words with digraphs include: *much, shock, them, then, there, think, what, with.*

Silent Consonants

Sometimes when two different consonants appear side by side, one of them is silent. In this story, words with silent consonants include: *Rick, snack.*

Sight Words

Sight words are those words that a reader must learn to recognize immediately—by sight—instead of by sounding them out. They occur with high frequency in easy texts. Sight words not included in the above categories are: *a, after, am, and, as, asked, at, could, do, from, good, have, he, I, in, is, it, look, my, no, of, on, out, over, play, said, she, the, to, too, up, us, want, was, would, you, your.*